Cinderella

Illustrations by J. L. MACIAS S.

Retold by JANE CARRUTH

Once upon a time there was a merchant who married again when his wife died. His new wife was a proud, cruel woman who hated the merchant's young daughter.

"Cinderella," she said, "will be her new name. Her place is in the kitchen, for she must do the work of a servant." The step-mother had two daughters. They were as proud and cruel as their mother, and very plain. At night they made poor Cinderella curl their hair and then sent her down to the kitchen to sleep on the stone floor, with only her faithful dog to keep her company as she slept.

Now, Cinderella, in her rags, was much prettier than the two Ugly Sisters. This made them very angry and, as the months passed, nothing she could do would please them. One day an invitation came from the palace to attend the Grand Ball the King was giving for his son, the Prince. Cinderella began to dream of going to the ball and this made the Sisters laugh at her.

"The Prince would never look at you in your rags!" they sneered. When at last the day came for the two Ugly Sisters to set out for the ball, Cinderella was at the washtub. "Oh, I do so long to be going to the Ball," she thought as she watched them go. And she sighed and began to cry because she was so sad at being left behind.

Still feeling sad, Cinderella set about the washing-up and it was then that something wonderful happened. Suddenly, there appeared before her the most beautiful lady she had ever seen. "I am your Fairy Godmother," said the beautiful lady.

"Do what I say and you will go to the Ball." Then she told
Cinderella to take a big pumpkin outside and fetch her the
mousetrap, which held six little mice. With a wave of her wand the
Fairy changed the pumpkin into a magnificent golden coach.

The six little mice became six handsome horses and some garden lizards found themselves changed into footmen. Cinderella gasped when she saw that she was no longer in rags but in a gorgeous dress of silk and satin embroidered with sparkling jewels and that on her feet were two dainty glass slippers, the prettiest in the world. "Was she dreaming?" she wondered.

"Remember," said the Fairy. "You must leave the Ball before the hour of midnight strikes or you will lose everything!"

As soon as Cinderella reached the palace, she was escorted into the ballroom. Almost at once, the king's son, the handsome young Prince, invited her to dance with him. All the ladies, who had hoped to dance with the Prince, were jealous.

"Who is she?" they whispered. "How lovely she looks! She must be a grand Princess. No wonder the Prince has eyes only for her!"

Cinderella was so happy dancing with the Prince that she forgot
the Fairy's warning. The palace clock was striking the hour of
twelve when she remembered. And with a cry of dismay she fled
from the ballroom and down the palace steps.

In her haste, she left behind one of her pretty glass slippers. The Prince tried to follow her, but he saw only a poor young girl in rags running down the street followed by six little mice.

Day after day, the Prince thought only of his mysterious Princess. At last he sent out a Proclamation that he would marry the girl who could wear the dainty glass slipper. His Messengers would take the slipper to every house in his kingdom.

When the Royal Messenger arrived at Cinderella's house, the two Ugly Sisters pushed and squeezed their feet into the slipper, but all in vain. But when Cinderella tried on the slipper it proved a perfect fit, and she was taken at once to the palace.

Cinderella and the Prince were married the very next day. Their wedding was the most magnificent the world had ever seen, and the happiest girl in the world was, of course, Cinderella.

Published in United States and simultaneously in Canada by Joshua Morri
431 Post Road East, Westport, CT
Printed in Be